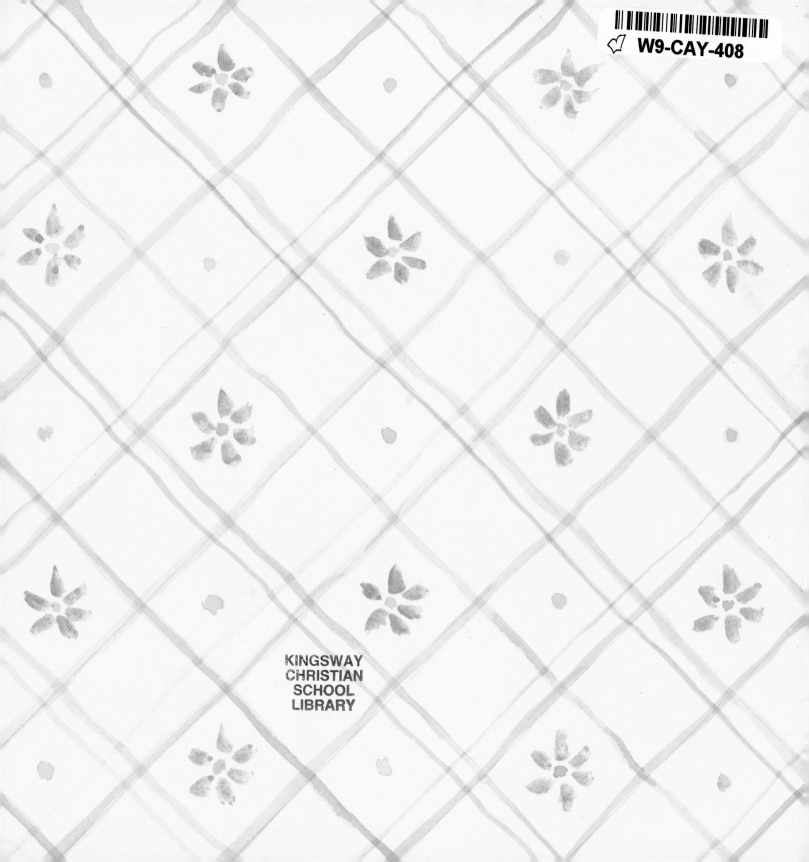

For Ian Michael, who is loved by his mama
—R.K.D.

For Colleen Brown—my mom!
—K.B.

Mama Loves
Text copyright © 2004 by Rebecca Kai Dotlich
Illustrations copyright © 2004 by Kathryn Brown
Manufactured in China by South China Printing Company Ltd.
All rights reserved.
www.harperchildrens.com

Library of Congress Cataloging-in-Publication Data
Dotlich, Rebecca Kai.
Mama loves / by Rebecca Kai Dotlich ; illustrated by Kathryn Brown.
p.   cm.
Summary: Some little pigs describe the many things and activities that
their mother loves and shares with them.
ISBN 0-06-029407-8 — ISBN 0-06-029408-6 (lib. bdg.)
[1. Mother and child—Fiction. 2. Family life—Fiction. 3. Pigs—Fiction.] I. Brown, Kathryn, ill. II. Title.
PZ7.D73735 Mam 2003
[E]—dc21
2002276252
Typography by Stephanie Bart-Horvath
1 2 3 4 5 6 7 8 9 10
❖
First Edition

Mama Loves

By Rebecca Kai Dotlich

Illustrated by Kathryn Brown

HarperCollinsPublishers

Mama loves
dancing in slippers.
Teapots of tea.
Reading the paper
and mornings
with me.

Mama loves
rain boots and rain hats.
Her face in the breeze.
Twirling umbrellas
and splashing
with me.

Mama loves
violets by windows.
Poppies and peas.
Lilacs and ladybugs
and listening
to me.

Mama loves
porch swings and
small things.
Butterflies and bees.
Postcards and poems
and reading
with me.

Mama loves
beach plum and starfish.
Shells from the sea.
Sand in her toes
and swimming
with me.

Mama loves
raking in rows.
Sprinkling new seeds.
Roses in baskets
and gardening
with me.

Mama loves
apples in autumn.
Sidewalks and leaves.
Sweaters and pumpkins
and walking
with me.

Mama loves
rivers and rope swings.
Her feet bare and free.
Hiking and biking
and being
with me.

Mama loves
cafés and coffee.
Cobblestone streets.
Chestnuts in brown bags
and shopping
with me.

Mama loves
tin cookie cutters.
Cupboards and keys.
Berries for baking
and cooking
with me.

Mama loves
bundling in blankets.
Buttons and beads.
Gingerbread squares
and sewing
with me.

Mama loves
listening to music.
Wind chimes in trees.
Hot milk and honey
and cuddling
with me.